Sir Squippel

Dorothea King

Summer had come and gone and the forest was enjoying a fine autumn. The oak tree had produced an exceptionally fine crop of acorns and the branches of the chestnut trees were weighed down with thick clusters of nuts.

On the outskirts of the forest the blackberry bushes were laden with plump ripe berries, and in the hedges the wild roses had gone, leaving behind their shiny red seed pods.

Autumn was the busiest time of the year for the animals who lived in the oak tree. They all worked from dawn till dusk gathering, sorting and storing the food which would have to last them through the winter months. There was never any time for fun and games and everyone tended to be rather short-tempered.

It was Sir Squirrel who came up with the idea of having a party. "Sort of a harvest celebration," he said to the others. "I of course, will organize it all."

"Will it be only for us? " asked Miss Mouse.

"Well, I had thought of inviting a few of my friend to join us," replied the squirrel. "Some of my more influential friends, that is."

"Sounds boring," said Master Rabbit scratching hi stomach.

"Not at all, my dear fellow, in fact you could lear a great deal from a grand social occasion such as this." The squirrel glanced at his watch. "Good gracious, is that the time? I really must be on my way. Lord Albert is expecting me for luncheon."

Sir squirrel knocked smartly on the door of Lord Albert's mansion and it was immediately opened by a young lady squirrel dressed in white mop-cap, black dress and white apron.

"His Lordship is expecting me," said Sir Squirrel and handed her his coat and hat.

He was shown into a drawing room, and sitting in a large leather armchair by the window was a rather elderly grey squirrel reading the morning paper.

"Good morning, your Lordship," said the squirrel. The grey squirrel looked up and peered at him through his monacle. "What's that you said — Oh, it's you, Squiffy, didn't recognised you for a minute."

Sir Squirrel really hated to be called Squiffy. He had been nicknamed it as a youngster, Lord Albert still insisted on using it.

The grey squirrel went over to a large grandfather clock and tapped the dial. "Blessed thing isn't working again," he said. "Never mind, never mind. I expect Agatha's already set lunch." He rubbed his hands together in anticipation. "It'll be roly-poly for afters and with any luck lashings of syrup."

They went into another room where a table was set for three. Lady Agatha had just finished arranging a large bowl of chrysanthemums and was obviously delighted to see the squirrel.

"Sir squirrel, how lovely of you to come," she said, and shook his hand warmly.

"The pleasure is all mine, your Ladyship," said the squirrel gallantly.

Lord Albert sat himself down in the chair at the head of the table and tucked a large napkin under his chin. "Come on, come on, let's get on with it," he said.

When they were all seated, Lady Agatha rang a tiny bell by the side of her plate and the maid brought in a tray on which were three bowls of soup and a basket of crusty rolls. After, they had a casserole of nuts and herbs which the squirrel declared delicious, and Lord Albert refused to eat. "Tastes like soggy cabbage," he glared at his wife.

When the dessert was brought in he was even more disgusted. "What, no roly-poly?" he roared. "Today is Wednesday, isn't it?"

"Well, yes dear," said his wife. "But roly-poly is so — so undignified when we have guests."

"In that case I'll make do with cheese and biscuits," he said grumpily and pushed the bowl of cold stewed apple away.

When they were all having coffee in the conservatory Sir Squirrel invited them to his harvest celebration. Lady Agatha accepted most graciously but his Lordship said he'd only come if roly-poly was on the menu. Sir Squirrel had no choice but to agree, after all, Lord Albert was the head of the Squirrel Association.

When he left the mansion Sir Squirrel went straight back home and proceeded to write invitations, making quite sure he left nobody out. After that he posted them in the Pigeon Post and hoped they would get to their destinations by the following morning. Which in fact they did.

When Miss Mouse got hers she rushed round to see the Hedgehog. "I've nothing to wear," she declared.

Mistress Hedgehog opened her invitation which was still lying on the mat and snorted as she read it. "Why we've got fancy invitations I'll never know, he told us all about it only yesterday."

A few seconds later there was a frantic hammering on the door and hedgehog opened it to find Master Rabbit clutching an envelope and looking most alarmed.

"I've had a letter," he gasped.

"Well, what does it say?" said Miss Mouse.

"I don't know, I can't read," replied the rabbit.

"Stupid animal," said the hedgehog taking the envelope from him. She glanced at the card inside and handed it back to the rabbit. "It's your invitation to Sir Squirrel's party," she said. "We've all had one."

"How do I know it's mine?" said the rabbit peering at the card. "It could be a mistake."

"It's your's because it's got your name on it, R A B B I T — !" she said spelling it out.

Master rabbit looked closely at the word she was pointing to and looked highly delighted. He had never seen his name written down before.

Once they had all decided they would go to the party Miss Mouse suggested they offer Sir Squirrel some help. After all they couldn't expect him to do all the cooking on his own.

Mistress Hedgehog and the mouse tapped gently on the squirrel's door and were amazed when he opened it wearing a large white hat and a long striped apron.

"Come on in, my dears," he said. "You're just in time to sample some of my acorns in red syrup."

"Ugghhh ..." said the hedgehog under her breath.

He led them through to his kitchen, which was remarkably neat and tidy, and gave them each a spoon to try his nut dessert. They both declared it delicious, but in truth Mistress Hedgehog did have great difficulty swallowing hers.

"We really came to see if we could be of any help," said Miss Mouse.

"Most kind of you both, but as you can see I have everything completely under control. There was just one thing though, can either of you make roly-poly?"

Miss Mouse said it was one of her best dishes and offered to make an especially large one.

After he had seen the mouse and the hedgehog to the door the squirrel got out his most advanced cookery books. On the night of the party he intended astounding everyone with his cooking.

With the party only three days away there was no time for Miss Mouse and Mistress Hedgehog to make anything new, and as it was going to be such an elegant occasion they decided to buy something ready-made from the shop.

Miss Mouse had no trouble finding something to fit and after trying a black dress — which made her look far too old, and a green silk

— which did nothing for her complexion, she finally settled on pure white chiffon with a pale pink sash.

Mistress Hedgehog had a
great deal more of a
problem, nothing seemed to
, either they were too short

or too tight.

After a frantic search
among the racks at the back
of the shop she finally found
a beautiful satin dress with a
matching stole which suited
her perfectly.

On the way home they met Master Rabbit. He was
carrying a large box but in spite of their pleading
was most secretive and refused to tell what was in it.

"What do you think it was?" said Miss Mouse to
her friend.

"Carrots no doubt," replied the hedgehog. "He's
such a stupid little animal."

On the afternoon of the party Sir Squirrel checked that everything was ready.

The table was set, fresh flowers filled the vases, the glasses sparkled and in the kitchen the food was all set out for what he referred to as "the party of the year."

The first guests to arrive were Miss Mouse and
Mistress Hedgehog. Graciously he welcomed them in
and handed out glasses of rose petal wine from a
silver tray.

After that came a rapid stream of people including
Lord and Lady Albert — whom the squirrel
announced with great pride.

Miss Mouse looked round the room, "Master Rabbit's not here yet," she whispered to the hedgehog. "What do you think could have happened to him?"

"Oh, don't worry about him," replied the hedgehog. "He's probably forgotten all about it."

They had all just sat down for dinner when there was a loud knock on the door. The squirrel opened it with a flourish to find the rabbit standing there. At first he didn't realize it was the rabbit but indeed it was.

He was wearing an immaculate black evening suit with matching cloak and on his head was a shiny top-hat. Carefully he removed the hat and handed it to the squirrel. Then he unbuttoned his white gloves and placed them inside the hat.

Sir Squirrel was absolutely dumbfounded, and as yet hadn't said a single word. Finally Master Rabbit removed his cloak and hung it on the squirrel's arm. "Good evening, old man," he said. "Remarkable weather we're having for this time of the year, don't you think?"

The hedgehog and the mouse gazed at each other in complete astonishment. Was it really him?

It was, and as Master Rabbit settled down at the table he gave them an enormous wink to prove it.

Everyone sat at the table waiting for the first course to appear. The squirrel had been out in the kitchen for ages and nobody could understand what could be taking him so long. After a while Mistress Hedgehog sensed that something was wrong and very quietly left her seat and went to the kitchen.

Never had she seen such a state in all her life. Pots and pans were everywhere, the smell of burning filled the air and in among the chaos was the squirrel, looking decidedly harassed.

"Mistress Hedgehog," he gulped. "You must help me, the soup boiled over, the souffle won't rise and just to make matters worse, I've put salt instead of sugar in the dessert."

Mistress Hedgehog was the ideal person to give help in a crisis. Grabbing an apron from the back of the door she quickly took control of the situation and banished the squirrel from the kitchen asking him to send Miss Mouse in immediately.

Nobody ever knew what kind of crisis had occurred in the kitchen that night. Sir Squirrel was a charming host for the rest of the evening and Miss Mouse and Mistress Hedgehog saved the day by producing one of the best meals anyone had ever tasted.

The crowning glory was Miss Mouse's roly-poly pudding of which Lord Albert had three helpings and promptly offered the squirrel a seat on the board of the Squirrel Association.

The party went on all through the night and as dawn crept gently over the forest the animals went very wearily, to their beds.

It really had been the party of the year!